EGG HOLDERS

Happy Easter Happy Easter

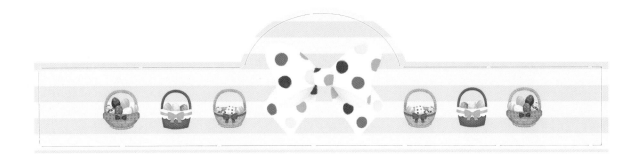

* Carefully press out each egg holder.
* Form a ring around an egg to get the correct size, and tape the ends together.
* Place your decorated Easter eggs in the rings!

The Sweetest Easter

By Andrea Posner-Sanchez
Illustrated by Daniela Massironi

A Random House PICTUREBACK® Book
Random House 🏠 New York

It's Easter! Peeps love smelling all the springtime flowers.

Peeps wear their Easter bonnets and have fun with friends.

Peeps look for butterflies.

Hop to it! The Peeps bunnies race through the grass.

Peeps go on an Easter egg hunt.

That's a lot of eggs!

That's a lot of Peeps! How many do you see?